LAVENDER

To Raphael and Thomas

LAVENDER
A JONATHAN CAPE BOOK 0 224 04729 9

Published in Great Britain by Jonathan Cape,
an imprint of Random House Children's Books

This edition published 2003

1 3 5 7 9 10 8 6 4 2

RANDOM HOUSE CHILDREN'S BOOKS
61-63 Uxbridge Road, London W5 5SA
A division of The Random House Group Ltd
RANDOM HOUSE AUSTRALIA (PTY) LTD
20 Alfred Street, Milsons Point, Sydney,
New South Wales 2061, Australia
RANDOM HOUSE NEW ZEALAND LTD
18 Poland Road, Glenfield, Auckland 10, New Zealand
RANDOM HOUSE (PTY) LTD
Endulini, 5A Jubilee Road, Parktown 2193, South Africa

THE RANDOM HOUSE GROUP Limited Reg. No. 954009
www.kidsatrandomhouse.co.uk

A CIP catalogue record for this book is available from the British Library.

Printed in China by Midas Printing Ltd

POSY SIMMONDS

LAVENDER

A Tom Maschler Book
JONATHAN CAPE • LONDON

Lavender lived on a bank
near the railway line.

She liked drawing and reading and quiet conversations with the hens.
Her brothers and sisters liked shouting and jumping out of trees
and balancing on wobbly things.
Lavender was often anxious.

No! **Don't!** It's dangerous!

Be careful!
Not so high!

You'll fall!

One day she was even more anxious than usual.
"Ssh! Listen!" she hissed. "Listen!"
Over the hill came a sound of bouncy
music, then laughing and barking,
and then a horrible smell.

Everyone dived into the nettles as a gang of foxes came huffing and puffing up the bank.

The rabbits crept out to have a better look
– all of them except...

Boo!!

But the foxes did nothing of the sort. They invited the rabbits to join their picnic.

The foxes explained that it was their first visit to the countryside.
They came from the town at the end of the railway line.
Their house was near a restaurant. A wonderful place to live!
Delicious things to eat right on the doorstep, night and day.
Pizza… pies… fries… doughnuts… bagels…

Then everyone – except Lavender, the Goose and the hens – ate pizza and danced to bouncy music, until it was time to go home.

The town foxes came the next weekend.
They invited everyone they met to come
and jump on their trampoline.
And everyone did.

Ooh! You must be a cow!

Well, almost everyone.

On their next visit, the foxes brought fudge cake,
popcorn and two inflatable sharks.
"Join us on the river!" they yelled.
And *nearly* everyone did.

When they arrived on their next visit, the foxes called out...

And Lavender jumped on the train.

Off went the train… down the valley…
through the long black tunnel… past
a wood full of furious weasels.
"I'm n-not scared," Lavender said
to herself. "I'm n-not s-scared!"

When the train stopped, everyone jumped off.
"Follow me!" shouted Chip. "This way to the party."
There was mud underfoot. There were prickles and bugs.
"What a horrible place!" grumbled the town foxes.

There were feathers and bones scattered about.
There was an almighty smell of fox.
"What a HORRIBLE, SCARY place!"
whispered everyone else.
Well, everyone, that is, except Lavender.

"I don't like it," said the sheep. "I'm off home."
"Let's get out of here," quacked the ducks.
"Yes, let's!" said the rabbits.

Lavender never saw them go. With her head down
she followed the foxes into the wood.

In you go,
little rabbit!
Welcome to
the party!

At the end of the path, a noise
of yapping and barking came
from a large tent.

!

The tent was *full* of country foxes who stared and muttered.

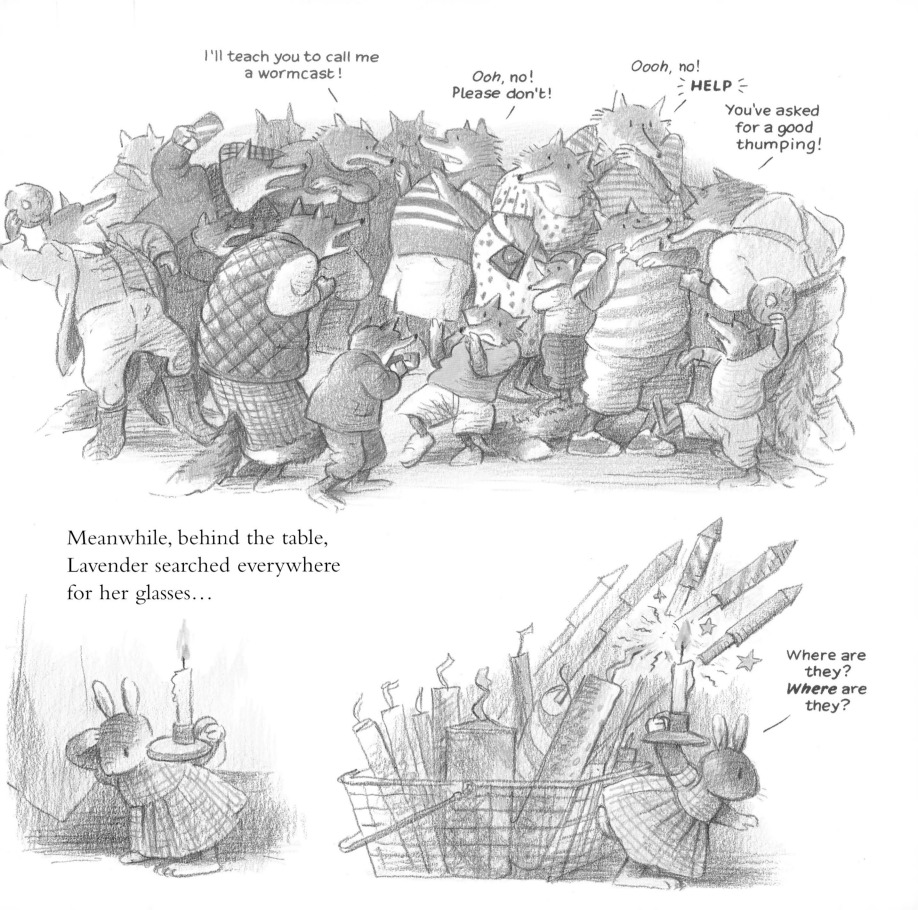

Meanwhile, behind the table,
Lavender searched everywhere
for her glasses…